MW00943048

KittyWood

THE KITTYTUBERS,
Book 3

by Darcy Pattison

Pictures by Nicole Standard

MIMS HOUSE
LITTLE ROCK, AR

For Haileigh, Bruce, Zeke, Gabe, Ash & Neona—
Follow your heart!

Mims House
1309 Broadway
Little Rock, AR 72202
mimshousebooks.com

Publisher's Cataloging-in-Publication Data

Names: Pattison, Darcy, author. | Standard, Nicole, illustrator.

Title: Kittywood / by Darcy Pattison ; illustrations by Nicole Standard.

Series: The Kittytubers

Description: Little Rock, AR: Mims House, 2021.

Summary: Angel Persian tries acting at each of the five major kennels in the hopes of becoming a Kittywood star.

Identifiers: ISBN: 978-1-62944-173-3 (Hardcover) | 978-1-62944-174-0 (pbk.) |978-1-62944-175-7 (ebook) | 978-1-62944-176-4 (audio)| LCCN 2020916111

Subjects: LCSH Cats--Juvenile fiction. | Internet videos--Juvenile fiction. | Online social networks--Juvenile fiction. | Family--Juvenile fiction. | BISAC JUVENILE FICTION / Performing Arts / Film | JUVENILE FICTION / Readers / Chapter Books

Classification: LCC PZ7.P27816 Fr 2020 | DDC [Fic]--dc23

Contents

FOR MORE ON THE KITTYTUBERS

MimsHouseBooks.com/Pages/KittyTubers

Other Chapter Books

by Darcy Pattison

THE ALIENS, INC. CHAPTER BOOK SERIES

Book 1: Kell, the Alien

Book 2: Kell and the Horse Apple Parade

Book 3: Kell and the Giants

Book 4: Kell and the Detectives

MimsHouseBooks.com/products/Kell

"I have only one rule in acting—trust the director and give him your heart and soul."
by Ava Gardner

EPISODE 1

Catnapping

> **WEATHER ALERT**
>
> Kittywood has an 80% chance of severe thunderstorms between 1:00 p.m. and 5:00 p.m. today.

Angel's tail twitches against the windowpane, then curls to rest beside her legs.

Behind her, black clouds swirl, churning and boiling. The storm strikes suddenly, rain lashing the windows.

She's an innocent fluff of fur silhouetted against the fury.

She catnaps.

The sky erupts with lightning bolts.

Flash!

Kittywood blinks in and out. The skyscrapers loom, black streaks against the eerie light.

The white kitten rests, motionless.

Unaware. Untroubled.

She catnaps.

A thunderclap.

Boom!

Angel shifts, rolling to her back, letting her legs sprawl. Comfortable. In deep sleep. Purring, purring, purring, she settles down.

Quiets.

She catnaps.

Rain lashes the window.

Pounding, crashing, pelting.

She catnaps.

Raining, raining, raining.

Raining, pittering, pattering.

She catnaps.

Pitter. Patter. Pit—pit—pit.

Rainbow!

She catnaps.

No!

She awakes!

She yawns.

Opens a blue eye.

Opens a copper eye.

She turns away from the camera to stare at the rainbow.

The colors—red, orange, yellow, green, blue, indigo and violet—wash over the white kitten.

She glows with color and life.

★★★

"I had this idea," Angel later explained about the video. "The director was unsure, but I wanted to try it.

"Here's the thing: People watch videos of a fireplace burning for hours. That's all it does. The fire burns and burns and burns. That's all it does. I just wondered, would they like to watch a kitten sleep?

"And then the weather forecast said a storm was coming. I realized a stormy background would be a striking contrast to a peacefully sleeping kitten. So we set it up!

"We took it from idea to finished video. What fun!

"That rainbow? That was pure luck. So, we edited the film to add the colored lights to look like rainbow colors were spilling onto my white fur."

The Directors

JUST KITTEN AROUND Joke

Q: Why did the cat sit on the computer?

A: To keep an eye on the mouse.

The top twenty kittens filed into Wiles Theater through the side doors, quiet, tails twitching nervously.

Angel and Jazz pushed forward to the first three rows of cushioned terraces. Only the top twenty kittens and a few of the Kittywood staff were here today. Behind them, other cat terraces and rows of seats for humans were empty, leaving the big auditorium dark and quiet.

This was an important meeting for the kittens trying to become KittyTube stars. They only had a month before some would get a KittyTube contract, and some would have to find other work. In a month, when the final kitten stars were chosen, the auditorium would be crowded with fans and tourists.

Jazz stepped daintily into the front row. But Angel gulped, shivering in the empty theater.

Under Angel's paws, the purple cushion fabric felt slick. She kneaded it with her claws, nervous energy making it hard to settle down. She circled and circled. She had injured herself in an acrobatics trick, but her legs felt fine now. Finally she sat with her tail curled around herself, as if it could corral her excitement.

Jazz settled beside her, looking regal. Her videos consistently topped the charts, so her calm didn't surprise Angel. Jazz had nothing to worry about.

Jazz whispered, "Quincy and PittyPat are two rows behind us."

Angel waved at her brother and sister. To their left were Rudy and the other members of the Ivory Bongo Harp Band, Curly and Maria.

The painted ceiling of Wiles Theater soared above the kittens' heads. A colorful ceiling mural showed the inventor of the cat-to-human speech translator, Arlo Porter Wiles. He was walking with three cats. This mural and theater, on the ground floor of Malachi-Glenys Kennels, attracted more tourists than any other sight in Kittywood except for the video cat stars themselves. Most tourists wanted to watch a videotaping. After that, they wanted to see the man who had given the translator to cats.

Wiles's invention was responsible for Kittywood. Visitors wanted to know more about him.

The theater darkened, and the kittens quieted.

A spotlight stabbed the dark to halo a cat who stood on the stage: MamaGrace.

Angel's heart swelled with pride. Her mother was so beautiful, despite her injured leg and scarred face. Before she even spoke, MamaGrace grabbed everyone's attention. She had an amazing stage presence, a cat who would never be ignored.

"Since you moved to the kittens' dorm at ten weeks old, you've been training with Majestic Kennels." MamaGrace's voice was soft, yet powerful. "The other kennels pay us a fee to be in charge of your education."

Jazz nudged Angel. "I didn't know that."

Angel whispered back, "You're Fox Kennels, right?"

Jazz nodded.

Everyone knew that Angel, Quincy, and PittyPat were born at Majestic Kennels—they were the children of Grace and Albert Persian, the Golden Ones. But Angel hardly knew which kennels her other friends called home.

MamaGrace paused for a moment and studied the gathered kittens. "This last month of your childhood, you'll each work with the directors from the other four kennels. They've planned special feature videos for you. Your videos this month still count toward your overall ranking on the kittens' leaderboard. But you must work with a variety of directors, camera operators, groomers, stage managers, and costume designers. By the end of the month," she said dramatically, "each kennel can offer only two contracts. Ten of you will become the newest video stars."

The kittens erupted in chatter, meows mixing with wails.

Angel told Jazz, "I don't want other groomers. Miss Tanya is the only groomer who understands what I need." Angel's pure white fur was hard to keep clean, and her grooming sessions were always longer than anyone else's.

Jazz held out a paw and licked it. "It's going to be a weird month."

"Attention!" MamaGrace said. She didn't use a microphone, yet her voice carried throughout the theater.

The kittens quieted.

"Let me introduce the directors of the five kennels of Kittywood." MamaGrace waved both paws and spun toward the stage behind her. Huge crimson stage curtains parted slowly. Five cats stood there with stiff front legs, heads thrown high. They stood in order from short to tall: a Singapura, a sphynx, a Bombay, an Abyssinian, and a Manx.

Angel's heart thumped against her chest. She'd met some directors at her parent's penthouse parties, but she'd never seen them all together. These five cats controlled the future of the kittens—indeed, of all of Kittywood. They chose the ideas and actors, and they made sure the videos reached viewers on KittyTube. Angel had to find the right director for her work, someone who might let her do more Underdog Cat videos or acrobatics videos, or someone who would inspire her to find other roles.

MamaGrace stepped to the side of the stage. "First," she said, "meet Ginger Singapura of Fox Kennels."

The spotlight spun wildly, then focused on a tawny, solid-colored Singapura cat who strutted forward. Like a human runway model, she walked by crossing her front legs with each step. Stopping, she rose on her hind legs and batted at the air.

A shock tingled down Angel's spine. She whispered to Jazz, "She looks like a kitten."

"Don't be fooled by her size," Jazz said with confidence. "Let me tell you, she's powerful. Her voice is small, but when she speaks, everyone listens."

Angel raised an eyebrow. If she could convince Director Ginger to let her do Underdog Cat, she'd be a valuable ally.

MamaGrace said, "Next is Stanley Sphynx of Majestic Kennels."

Angel sighed in relief. At least this director was familiar. The intense spotlight shimmered on his hairless body, revealing soft folds of skin. He stepped forward as if walking on eggshells. He ran Majestic—and the kittens' dorm—with an iron will. If Angel could choose, she'd stay with Majestic. But maybe that was because it was familiar. She should give the other kennels a chance to woo her.

Next, a medium-sized sleek panther-like cat glided into the spotlight.

MamaGrace said, "Meet Raquel Bombay of Cardinal Kennels."

Raquel's green eyes flashed as she looked over the audience of kittens like a lioness protecting her territory.

Would this director be interested in my acrobatics tricks? Angel wondered.

"Next up," MamaGrace said, "is Esha Abyssinian, director of Malachi-Glenys Kennels."

An Abyssinian with burnt sienna fur trotted forward to speak to the crowd, the first director to say anything. "Good evening. I'm so excited to get to know you kittens. It's a great day for you and for us. We're going to have FUN this month, don't you think?"

The kittens erupted with cheers.

Angel grinned at Director Esha and joined the cheers. She hoped the month would be fun. Working with each kennel could be fun—or very, very difficult. At least Director Esha was starting with encouragement.

"Meet Domingo Manx of Wells Brothers!" MamaGrace said.

Director Domingo, a Manx cat with long back legs and no tail, stomped into the spotlight and bowed. He was a tricolor: inky black, alabaster white, and sunset orange. He towered over Ginger Singapura and Stanley Sphynx and was much larger than Directors Esha and Raquel.

Angel stiffened her front legs and lifted her chest, trying not to be intimidated. She needed to be strong and confident when she worked for each director.

The stage lights came up, and the five directors stood once again in a line. The room suddenly seemed too small. Angel sucked in a breath, staring at her future. She just had to convince one director to take a chance on her. Her videos had strong views, so she was hopeful. This month, though, it was more about finding a home. Where would she feel most comfortable with a studio's workplace? Which studio would have a vision for her work?

Her eyes traveled back and forth among the directors. From black to sienna to tricolor to hairless. From graceful to strong, from quiet to leading a cheer.

Would she find a home?

MamaGrace returned to the stage's center: "When you get back to the kittens' dorm, check your email. I've sent a schedule to each of you. It will explain where you'll go tomorrow and every day after that for thirty days. Please don't ask me to change them because it's too complicated."

Another wave of chatter washed through the theater.

Thoughtful, Angel leaned to Jazz and said, "By next month, we'll be cats, not kittens."

The Kennels

JUST KITTEN AROUND Joke

Q: What has the fur of a cat, the whiskers of a cat, ears of a cat, a tail of a cat, but is not a cat?

A: A kitten.

Kittens crammed into Jazz and Angel's room, chittery and jittery.

"Quiet!" Jazz yelled.

Angel shuddered at the crush of kittens and finally leaped onto the broad windowsill. She bared her teeth at any other kitten who tried to join her. Warily, they gave her space.

"Who's from Cardinal Kennels? What can you tell us about it?" Jazz asked. This meeting was her idea. She'd invited other kittens to discuss the kennels saying, "We need information so we'll be prepared and can do our job better."

One by one, kittens shared what they knew about their home kennels.

Curly, the Singapura kitten who played bongos for the Ivory Bongo Harp Band, climbed onto Jazz's computer table so she could be seen. "Cardinal Kennels is a happy place," she said.

Angel leaned forward to hear Curly's soft voice.

"Director Raquel never discourages or calls you out," Curly said. "You need to do a good job, of course, but most important, you must get along."

Jazz asked, "On the kennel's leaderboard, where does Cardinal Kennels rank?"

"Third," Curly said. "It's a solid position."

Angel turned to look out the window, frowning. She'd like a happy, encouraging kennel, but she didn't need third place. Looking around, she wondered who came from Wells Brothers Kennels, which was always last.

"Next?" Jazz said.

Angel decided to get it over with. She stood and puffed out her chest. "I was born here at Majestic Kennels. You know Director Stanley and our staff, so I won't say much except this: we're the top-ranked kennel. Always have been. Always will be."

Kittens jeered at her good-naturedly, but Quincy and PittyPat nodded approvingly. They understood Angel's love for Majestic Kennels. It had been good for their parents' careers and had been a good place to grow up. She could see herself going to another kennel, but only if it was the right place for her career.

Jazz just shrugged. "Next?"

A tricolored cat wove through the crowd to the front. Angel recognized Ismo Bobtail, a kitten she didn't know very well.

Ismo said, "Malachi-Glenys Kennels is slow and methodical about everything. Director Esha doesn't chase fads."

"She's great," said Blondie, an Abyssinian with a following for her chase-cat videos.

"We don't pay top dollar for anything. Our stars don't make the highest salaries. But Malachi-Glenys always ranks as the number two kennel. If you want a long, steady career, it's the place for you."

"That's so different from my home kennel," Jazz said. "Fox Kennels loves to set trends, not just follow them. Director Ginger is very competitive."

Ismo pawed the air. "Then why is Malachi-Glenys always number two and Fox is number four?"

Jazz looked down and shook her head. Looking up again, she said slowly, as if she was trying to figure it out, "Don't know. Somehow, Director Ginger doesn't quite understand the human audience. What will they want to watch? Director

Ginger makes wild guesses, and sometimes we make a video that goes viral. But more often, she's wrong. Still Fox Kennels is a fun place with something new all the time. If you get bored easily and you don't care about the rankings, it's the place for you."

Rudy jumped up beside Curly on the computer table. A black-and-white Devon Rex kitten, his big ears flicked back and forth. "I'm from Wells Brothers. We're small. We're last. And we don't care. We take life easy. Mr. Wiles gave us the translator to make our lives better, not to send cats on a wild rat chase to be number one. We turn out good videos and have a strong following." Rudy shrugged. "Or at least that's what Director Domingo always says: 'Enjoy life! It's too short to worry about fame.'"

Oh, thought Angel, *that's why Rudy was so laid back at first.* Until he started the Ivory Bongo Harp band, Rudy had just drifted along.

They talked long into the night, telling stories of their home kennels. But in the end, it didn't matter what they wanted. What mattered was the kind of KittyTube star that each director needed.

Angel worried and worried. Would she find a home? Would she become a KittyTuber?

EPISODE 2

Underdog Cat Protects the City

Underdog Cat stands on the roof terrace of Majestic Kennels wearing a simple costume of wrist bands and an eye mask. Behind her, the sunset streaks the sky orange. She is a stark silhouette against the brilliant clouds.

Below her, Kittywood comes alive. Streetlights created pools of light for the dark streets. Along the commercial streets, neon signs invite hungry cats to their favorite restaurants. Daylight-bright lights glare onto the river docks so that barges can still load and unload. The hustle and bustle—the city is in motion, cats and humans moving with purpose, car horns beeping along crowded roads.

Underdog Cat spreads her front paws wide as if to hug the city. It is her town, her home. She'll do anything to protect it! She isn't important enough for a signal like the Bat-Signal that calls Batman. Maybe someday. But she likes to stand on the top of Majestic Kennels in case someone needs her.

A scream splits the night air.

Underdog Cat scans the area. It sounded like someone was hurt badly.

There!

Outside a restaurant, a human is yelling, "Thief!"

A white cat scampers away from the restaurant.

(CUT! That's a wrap on this scene. Let's move to the street for the rest of this episode.)

Underdog Cat appears to fly down from the top of Majestic Kennels. She lands right on top of the exotic white cat. (It's Isobelle, the Exotic cat. She's loving her new job in advertising. But like any cat, she can come back for a cameo role.)

Underdog Cat and the white thief cat struggle, both wailing and slashing sharp claws at each other. They roll, and the thief pops up and dashes away. Underdog Cat leaps, stretching out her claws and reaching forward until she snags the other cat's back leg.

The thief yelps, stumbles and rolls. Up instantly, she whirls to slash at Underdog Cat, who dances sideways and then lunges back to trip up the thief again.

This time, the thief lands with a thump and is still.

Underdog Cat stands over her, making sure she doesn't get away.

The restaurant owner arrives. "You stopped her! She stole everything in our cash drawer."

Underdog Cat notices a white pouch slung across the thief's back. It's stuffed with money.

Police arrive and give the money back to the restaurant owner. An ambulance arrives, and hands gently pick up the thief to put her on a stretcher. She's stirring now, eyes opening. The ambulance disappears with its siren wailing, while Underdog Cat explains everything to the police.

"She'll go to jail, for sure," the policeman says. "Thanks for your help."

Kittywood is safe again because Underdog Cat watches the city, protecting it. Underdog Cat saves the day. Again.

EPISODE 3

Wrecking the Ivory Bongo Harp Band

JUST KITTEN AROUND Joke

Q: Why did the kittens ask for a piano, a bongo set and a harp?

A: They wanted to make some mew-sic.

Rudy paces the length of the piano keyboard. He lifts his legs high, each step a deliberate strike of a note. His head bounces in a gentle rhythm.

The camera pulls back to show muscled men.

Rudy nods at the men and hops to the floor. The men squat, wrapping long arms around the piano. They lift it onto the bed of a pickup truck.

One man climbs into the cab, starts the truck and drives away. He turns out of the driveway—too fast! Oh, no!

The piano tips.

Rudy's mouth is wide. He races toward the truck.

The piano tips even more. Top-heavy, it falls.

Smashes onto the pavement.

88 white and black keys scatter onto the ground.

Rudy stops. Shock and anger fill his eyes.

On a raised stage, Curly plays a bongo solo, paws beating in rhythm.

Three bongos, tight drumheads. The beat pulses, making Curly's head bounce.

The camera pulls back to show muscled men.

Curly nods at the men and hops to the floor.

The men squat, wrapping long arms around each bongo. They lift each one onto the bed of a pickup truck.

One man climbs into the cab, starts the truck and drives away. He turns out of the driveway—too fast! Oh, no!

The bongos tip.

Curly's mouth is wide. She races toward the truck.

The bongos tip even more. Top-heavy, they fall.

Smash onto the pavement.

Drumheads scatter onto the ground. Torn leather and wood.

Curly skids to a stop. Shock and anger fill her eyes.

On a raised stage, Maria plucks her harp, a sweet melody.

Harp strings vibrate. Maria closes her eyes, nodding at the notes that rise and fall.

The camera pulls back to show muscled men.

Maria puts her paws on the harp strings to still them. She nods at the men and hops to the floor.

The men squat, wrapping long arms around the harp. They lift it onto the bed of a pickup truck.

One man climbs into the cab, starts the truck and drives away. He turns out of the driveway—too fast! Oh, no!

The harp tips.

Maria's mouth is wide. She races toward the truck.

The harp tilts even more. Top-heavy, it falls...

...but coming down from heaven, three angel kittens swoop in—watch them in slow-motion—wings beating, halos glowing, paws reaching.

They catch the harp.

They gently lower it to the ground.

The angel kittens straighten and look around. One angel walks to a pile of piano keys swept against the curb. She waves a paw. The piano keys and broken bits of wood shiver, wiggle, and quiver. Suddenly Rudy's piano stands there, whole again.

Another angel walks to the scattered bits of wood and leather. She waves a paw. The drumheads and broken bits of wood rattle, clatter, and clink. Suddenly Curly's bongos stand there, whole again.

The angels carefully pick up each instrument and fly them back to the stage. They beckon to the musicians.

Rudy, Curly and Maria mount the stage steps. The Ivory Bongo Harp Band plays. The harp's melody weaves in and out of the piano's trills and grace notes, while the bongo binds everything into a celebration of life. A promise that broken things can be made whole again.

★★★

"I had this idea," Rudy later explained about the video. "Everyone thought it was crazy to have our instruments fall apart. But I insisted that we try."

"Of course, we used old instruments, not our good ones. Miss Emily, our favorite designer, made the angel costumes. And I thought the piano keys on the pavement would be an amazing image.

"It's a thrill to see ideas come to life.

"And best of all, the song from this video is popular. How popular is it? When Angel and I went for our morning walk, Director Domingo ran past. He was humming the song! Our song! My song!"

Rudy and Angel

JUST KITTEN AROUND Joke

Q: Which day of the week do cats love the most?

A: Caturday.

Angel yawned and stepped off the elevator. She'd awakened at dawn, ready to be up and moving. So she'd come downstairs to check the leaderboards. Turning right, she trotted silently to them.

The glowing red letters made her stomach flip with happiness. Her "A Kitten Sleeps in a Storm" video had been number one last week, and usually a video dropped quickly. But it was sticking at number two!

"What's your rank?"

Rudy stood beside Angel, his black eyes like saucers in the dim room.

Angel said, "Well, you're number one with that 'Wrecking the Ivory Bongo Harp Band' video. Congratulations!" It was easier to congratulate others when her own work was doing well.

Rudy looked from the leaderboard to Angel. "Number two! Wow! It didn't drop far. Congratulations to you."

Happiness filled Angel with a mischievousness. She and Jazz always play-wrestled when there was good news. She whirled and bumped her chest against Rudy.

But Rudy fell heavily and was slow getting up.

A pang struck Angel's heart. Rudy was smaller than Jazz, so maybe Angel had hit him with too much force. "Oh! I'm sorry! Are you okay?"

Rudy stood with his head hung low. His shoulders shivered, as if shaking off a pesky bug. "I need to talk with someone. Do you have time? Can we walk around the Catnip Meadow?"

"Sure. Breakfast isn't served for another hour."

Rudy shook himself and seemed to recover. Together, they ran to the street and scampered toward the Catnip Meadow. Angel watched Rudy sideways. Perhaps he wasn't feeling as well as he said. She was so worried about Rudy that she ran full speed into another cat and fell backward from the impact.

From her back, Angel looked upward and groaned. "Oh, so sorry, sir."

Standing over her was Director Domingo, the large Manx cat from Wells Brothers.

"Sorry," said Director Domingo. "I was thinking and not paying attention. Are you okay? Did I hurt you?"

Angel pushed up to stand and shook herself from nose to tail-tip. Finally she said, "I'm okay."

Eyebrows pinched, Director Domingo glanced from Angel to Rudy. "Do I know you?"

Rudy nodded. "I'm from Wells Brothers. My parents are Logan and Lina."

Angel said, "I'm Angel Persian, daughter of Grace and Albert."

"Ah," Director Domingo said. "I know both of you." He nodded to Rudy and said, "What do you hear from your uncle Eli? He was one of our best actors. That Flash Feline character was so popular."

"Wait!" Angel whirled to face Rudy. "Flash is your uncle!"

Rudy shrugged and nodded.

Angel's jaw sagged in shock. Her brother, Quincy, had watched so many Flash videos that she had them memorized.

To Director Domingo, Rudy said, "He's fine. Retirement is easy for him. While working, he earned enough to buy a small cottage with an herb garden. He sells herbs at the farmer's market most weekends."

Director Domingo sighed. "Good. It was so sad."

Rudy said, "Yes, but he's fine."

The Manx cat shook himself, dancing on his tiptoes. "Well, I need to finish my run. I'll be seeing each of you later this month, eh?"

Rudy and Angel nodded, but Director Domingo had already darted away.

Angel rounded on Rudy. "Why didn't I know about your uncle?"

"You never asked about my family."

"Well, I talk about my family all the time. Why don't you talk about yours?"

Rudy just shrugged and trotted down the path after the Manx cat. "Let's run a bit. Then I need to talk."

Angel followed him, curiosity welling up. Something was going on, but she could wait till he was ready. The dew was still on the grass, cool and inviting. They trotted side by side, enjoying the soft morning air.

As they ran, though, Rudy started breathing heavily.

Angel stopped, but Rudy ran on, so she had to catch up.

Finally Rudy stopped at a water fountain, his head hanging, his breath labored. He kicked out his hind legs as if working out a muscle twitch.

Angel lapped a drink, and then sat in a ray of sunshine. Wrapping her tail around her, she demanded, "Sit. Talk."

Rudy nodded, his black ears twitching now. But he didn't settle down beside her. He lapped a drink, walked around the fountain, sat beside her, rose up, walked around the fountain the opposite way—his legs did that high-stepping gait that he used on the piano. He settled beside a carved mushroom and propped his front legs on it.

Angel waited patiently. She couldn't imagine what was so serious.

At last, Rudy said, "You ever see a Flash Feline video?"

"Every one of them! We loved Flash; he's a classic. Well, Quincy liked him best and wanted to be a Flash. But he's too slow. Likes his food too much."

"Ever wonder why he retired?"

Light reflected from the water fountain played across Rudy's face. "No," Angel said. "When you're a kitten, you don't worry about retirement. Do you?"

Rudy's eyes flashed darkly. "No." He paused a long moment. "Except…"

Then silence.

Angel's heart thumped. Rudy needed to say something but couldn't. What was going on?

"Except?" Angel said softly.

"Did you watch the 'Wrecking of the Ivory Bongo Harp Band' video?" Rudy said.

Angel nodded. "I loved the angel cats saving the day. Did you get Miss Emily to do the costumes? It looked like something she once designed for me."

Rudy nodded absently, facing the hypnotic babble of the fountain. "Yes, Miss Emily said they'd been for you. But you didn't buy them, so she just redid them for us." He turned to her. "Do you think I did a good job?"

Angel wanted to shake Rudy, to make him talk. But he had to do it his way. She took a deep breath and forced herself to relax. She laid her head on her paws, her gaze focused on Rudy. With her odd-colored eyes, she stared, hoping for a soul-connect with him.

Rudy broke the gaze first, his chin drooping almost to the ground.

Angel sat up sharply. "Rudy! What's wrong?"

"That's what I'm trying to tell you. I saw a doctor late yesterday afternoon. I have Devon Rex myopathy, just like Uncle Eli. It's why he retired from his Flash Feline character. My days are numbered."

"What?" Angel's mind whirled. "Wait, explain. What is this Devon Rex thing?"

"My-OP-athy," Rudy said. "Some Devon Rex get it, some don't. But it runs in my family."

Angel's heart felt like it stopped. She forced herself to suck in air. "What does it do?"

"My muscles are getting weak. My head bounces, and I can't stop it. I walk funny, with high steps."

Angel replayed Rudy's video in her mind. When he was walking on the keyboard, his head bounced. But that was part of the act, Rudy keeping time to the music. Wasn't it? He danced on the keyboard with high steps. But that was just showmanship. Right?

"How bad?" Angel croaked.

"No way to know. It begins about three to six months old and gets worse until a cat is a year old. For some, it stabilizes at a year old and never gets worse. For Uncle Eli, though, it just kept getting worse and worse. He was only three and a half years old when he retired."

"Wow! But what an amazing career he had in that time! His videos are KittyTube classics." Angel wanted to protect Flash Feline's reputation, wanted to protect her friend. She gulped hard, holding back tears. But she couldn't defend him, could she? When someone got sick, you couldn't stop it.

Rudy sank down to rest his chin on the stone mushroom.

"When will you tell Director Stanley?" Angel asked. Would they let Rudy go through Contract Day? Or would he have to retire before his career even started?

Rudy murmured something so low that Angel had to ask, "What? Say it again."

Rudy whispered, "I don't think I'll tell him."

Angel's eyes grew wide with shock. She froze, unable to speak.

"My health isn't any of his business," Rudy said, defiant now, lifting his chin to stare at the fountain.

The water splashed and sprayed, light catching water drops like hard, glittery diamonds. Angel's heart squeezed, full of grief that her friend faced this horrible illness. And outrage that he would try to hide it.

"It may never get bad." Rudy's jaw clamped shut, and he had to force out words. "Sometimes it's very mild and the Devon Rex will look normal to everyone but family."

Angel swallowed and licked her lips. "But your uncle..."

"I just wanted someone to know..." Rudy's words flowed as if a dam had burst. "So I could tell someone that I'd had a bad day or that my legs hurt or whatever. I thought maybe we were good enough friends that I could tell you, and you'd understand, and not judge me or anything. This band—I need it. I'll figure out something so the band doesn't get hurt by my illness. I just need to make it through the next few weeks. The band needs that contract. Needs it! Did you know that Maria is from Wells Brothers, too? Maybe Director Domingo will take a serious look at the band because two of us are Wells Brothers. And our 'Wreck' video is the top video this week. Maybe Majestic will look at us seriously. No one has done a band like this for KittyTube before, or a contract for a band, and Director Stanley was just saying how awesome it was that we figured out something new—"

He stopped.

Angel thought, *I figured out something new. Rudy being a piano cat was my idea.* She shook her head slightly. Not that it mattered where the idea came from. Rudy was right that the band was new and fresh and different. The band's views had shot sky high, which meant any kennel could recruit them.

"But..." Angel stopped. Could Rudy keep this secret? Should he keep it secret? Should she?

Rudy shoved off the stone mushroom. Looking at it, he said, "It's more comfortable if I keep my front paws and chin raised on something like that." He let his head wag from side to side like a Komodo dragon. "I can keep this quiet for a month. I have to." He shivered, letting his fur ruffle from nose to tail, as if he were shaking off the conversation. With a lighter voice, he said, "Hey, want to meet and walk the Catnip Meadow in the mornings? This will be a crazy month working at the different kennels. Maybe we both need to talk."

"Sure," Angel said. "Jazz likes to sleep late, but I can't. And it's nice to be outside before working inside all day."

"I'm hungry. Let's go to the cafeteria." Rudy trotted back toward Majestic Kennels.

Following, Angel studied his gait. It wasn't awkward, and it wasn't jerky or rough. Instead, it was just...not quite smooth. No one would know he had a problem unless he told them.

Or unless she told them.

The thought made her growl.

Rudy had grabbed the top spot this week with his "Wreck" video. He didn't say it, but he expected the band to be offered a contract at Majestic. Jazz probably already had a contract with Majestic in her pocket, with all her top videos.

Where did that leave Angel? Each kennel could only offer two contracts to kittens. Would Majestic offer a contract to her or to Rudy's band?

If—and this was just an "if"—she told the Director Stanley about Rudy's illness, it would protect Majestic, who needed every cat to contribute to overall views. If she didn't tell, Rudy's band might take away her Majestic contract. But if she told, Rudy would never forgive her.

Rudy said he wouldn't tell anyone about his illness.

Should she tell?

Angel wanted to run to MamaGrace or DaddyAlbert and ask for advice. But they cared too much about Majestic, and she knew what they'd do. Rudy would have no chance if she talked to them. This time, she had to figure it out for herself.

Unhappy, she stopped to roll in the catnip, to cover herself with the heavenly scent, hoping it would distract her. Instead, she paused, upside down, her spine deep in the catnip and cried silently to the achingly beautiful blue sky: *What am I going to do?*

Wells Brothers Video

"That's it?" Angel stood on the film stage at the Wells Brothers studio. It was her first video for another kennel, and she'd expected an exciting script. Instead, they'd just asked her to jump from a man's shoulder and perform a single flip.

"Sure," Director Domingo said. "It'll be a great video." The tall Manx nodded to the camera operator, who started turning off lights and cameras.

"But I did nothing different. It's exactly like the acrobatics video I did for Majestic Kennels." This was all wrong. Angel's stomach cramped at the thought of releasing a video that copied a previous video. What were they thinking?

"Trust me. Our film editors will do amazing things with it. You'll never recognize it."

"What does that mean?"

The director turned on her, his face so close that Angel could count his whiskers, which quivered in anger. "Have you ever watched Wells Brothers videos?"

Stepping backward, she said, "No." She'd only watched kitten videos, and those all came from Majestic Kennels. "Well, only classics like Flash Feline."

The director rolled his eyes and shook his head. "Kittens. They'll be the death of me." He turned away but spun back. "Okay." His voice was harsh, the frustration lying just below the surface. "Here's your homework. You either do this, or you don't work for me tomorrow. Go home and watch five videos, one from each kennel. Be ready to tell me the differences. How does each kennel approach a video in a unique way?"

"What?" Angel wrinkled her nose. Cat videos were cat videos. The cat or kitten star each had a style, of course, a signature look or typical type of video. Quincy, for example, always did a food video. How could a kennel make a different sort of video? Quincy would always be Quincy, just like Angel would always be Angel. Repeating an acrobatics video was crazy.

The director's tailless rump swayed as he swept out of the room without a backward glance.

Tears filled Angel's eyes. She didn't understand this director. What did he want from her? She blinked to stop the tears and stalked from the studio.

Okay. She had homework.

But she wouldn't watch five videos. She'd watch twenty-five.

The Video Binge Party

JUST KITTEN AROUND Joke

Q: What does a cat have that no other animal has?

A: Kittens.

Angel, Jazz, PittyPat, Quincy, Rudy, Curly, and Maria curled up together to watch videos. They binge-watched twenty-five videos, five from each kennel.

At the end, silence reigned as they considered.

Finally Angel said, "Well, Majestic has great story lines."

"But for post-production editing," Rudy said, "you can't beat Wells Brothers. They add special effects, reversals, or slow motion. It adds a lot."

Quincy agreed. "I love what they do in post-production. It takes a great film editor to do that. Jane Manx runs that, doesn't she?"

Rudy nodded.

"She must be amazing," Quincy said. "Think about my video of eating a spider. They could make the spider walk in my mouth, then reverse it to back out. In and out. That would make it a creepier video."

Angel nodded, surprised that she agreed. The Wells Brothers effects did take a normal video to another level.

PittyPat leaned forward to tap the screen with a soft paw. "You know what surprises me about Malachi-Glenys is that they are perfect in timing releases. Just when you want a summer video, they've got a great one. When it's back-to-school time, they do a perfect video. And then they have all this backlog of seasonal videos. It's a brilliant way to produce videos."

"I loved their holiday videos," Curly said. "Do you think they'd want holiday music videos?"

Rudy's eyebrows went up. "Good question!"

Maria said, "Cardinal likes big names. They have great actors, but they like to bring in a big name for a cameo. They do a bit part, but that helps to sell the video."

"That's smart," PittyPat said. "It builds up their actors to be seen with the big names."

"Even though I'm from Fox Kennels," Jazz said. "I feel like they can't hit the bullseye. They try something new—they love trendy ideas—and it works. But they hit to the side of the target. That means another kennel comes in, perfects it, and gets the most views."

Quincy said, "I love the new ideas. That last video—the water sports one—was amazing! Did you like that, PittyPat?"

"Yes!" PittyPat said. "Volleyball in a pool! How great is that?"

"But think," Angel said. "Next month, Majestic will do water sports but will add a great story to it. They'll get more views."

They looked at each other, and Angel said what they were all thinking. "Every kennel is so different. I thought Majestic's way was the only way. But now—I don't know."

"I think," Jazz said, "that means we're growing up."

Quincy started it with a chuckle, and then PittyPat gave a snort, and Curly pounded her pillow, and then they were all laughing.

"Growing up?" Angel said. "Not us!"

EPISODE 4

Acro-ba-kits

The white cat stands on the shoulder of a tall, lanky man dressed in black. She stares into the camera, an intense gaze—Oh, look! A blue eye and a copper eye!—that grabs the viewer's heart.

She leaps. Her white fur floats. She tucks her head. In slow motion, she rolls—a perfect flip—then stretches her claws toward the floor.

VOICEOVER: Hey, want to see it backwards?

The kitten's feet touch the floor,
then she unwinds,
going backward,
reversing the flip,
fur f-l-o-a-t-i-n-g,
and then settling down as she lands on the man's shoulder.

She soul-connect stares at the camera.

VOICEOVER: Again?

The kitten stares,
leaps,
rolls,
touches down,
reverses upward,
unrolls,
and lands on the man's shoulders.

VOICEOVER: Double-time!

Stare, leap, roll, touch,
reverse, unroll, shoulder,
stare, leap, roll, touch,
reverse, unroll, shoulder.
Stare.
Stare.
Stare.
Soul-connect!

TALK IT OUT

Jazz and Angel

JUST KITTEN AROUND Joke

Q: Why did the cat put the letter M into the freezer?

A: Because it turns "ice" into "mice"!

Jazz stood in front of the mirror tugging at the Hawaiian grass skirt. It fit around her front legs, but she kept stepping on it.

"Miss Emily will have to come and cut it shorter," Jazz said.

"But I love the coconut swimsuit top," Angel said. "It suits you."

"Ha!" Jazz snorted. "Would you tell me the truth?"

Angel raised both paws in surrender. "Of course! I only tell the truth."

Jazz wriggled out of the skirt and started trying on a frog outfit.

While Jazz's head was hidden in the middle of the green material, Angel put her paws over her mouth and laughed to herself. But when Jazz's face popped out, Angel was ready. "Okay, here's the truth. You know that I wouldn't wear any of the things you wear. But it works for you! You're the top kitten, and you've been the top kitten for months. The Hawaiian outfit will be another winner."

Jazz adjusted the frog face so that huge eyes sat on top of her head. Her own eyes peered out of the frog's mouth.

Smothering a laugh, Angel said, "But I'm not so sure you make a good frog."

Jazz bent her legs and then leaped. She frog-leaped around the room.

Angel finally gave in, laughing and laughing. "You know what?" she struggled to say. "That will play well on KittyTube."

Jazz pulled off the costume and climbed onto the windowsill. The afternoon sun streamed in. Angel joined her, and they sank into a half doze. They'd both had busy days. With an hour before supper, it was a good time for a catnap. The windowsill was warm and comfortable.

Drowsily, Jazz said, "So what are you working on these days?"

"I'm doing acrobatics, and June Manx is editing them in fun ways. But what I want to work on is Underdog Cat."

"Why? Last week you were so excited by the acrobatics."

"I love the acrobatics. It's too limited, though. Cat bodies can't do all the tricks that Captain Piper wants to teach us. I've tried. Single and double flips from any height are easy. But the twists and harder tricks—I just can't do them. Underdog Cat seems to have more possibilities."

"So do Underdog Cat."

"It's not that easy. I need to work on the story of Underdog Cat."

"Like what?"

"Superheroes have stories about how they became a superhero. Like Batman's parents getting killed, or Superman's parents sending him as a baby to Earth just before their planet, Krypton, explodes. Or Flash Feline getting zapped by electricity during the construction of Wells Brother's studios."

Jazz yawned. "Good idea. What's Underdog Cat's story?"

"But that's just it. I don't have any ideas."

"You know who does have ideas? Rudy. He came with me to the Doodle Studio and talked with Miss Emily. They decided I needed outfits for things like the beach and the army—including a helmet. They also agreed on a snowman outfit, a lamb, a top hat and dancing shoes, and a chef's hat and apron.

Rudy suggested this Hawaiian grass skirt and the frog. He has great ideas."

Angel nodded slowly. She and Rudy were walking around the Catnip Meadow a couple mornings a week. Next time, she'd ask his advice on Underdog Cat. She needed as many ideas as possible.

TALK IT OUT

The Underdog Cat Character

JUST KITTEN AROUND Joke

Q: When is it bad luck to see a black cat run across your path?

A: When you're a mouse.

"I need help with my Underdog Cat character," Angel said.

Rudy rolled around in the lush catnip. Instead of running on the sidewalk surrounding the Catnip Meadow, Angel had suggested they walk straight across to enjoy the catnip. Rudy rolled right and left but didn't roll over completely. Angel's feet twitched as she mentally tried to help the small cat complete the roll. Not long ago, he could've done a somersault in the catnip. But some mornings, it was hard for him to even walk until after he had loosened up with stretches. He pushed through the days, not letting his illness show.

But Angel could see that it was getting worse. When would he tell Director Stanley?

Rudy sat up. "Character. We can work on character. What do you need?"

"You know," Angel said. "Things like where Underdog Cat came from. Wonder Woman came from a hidden island. The Fantastic Four were blasted with cosmic rays. Things like that."

"Let's walk and talk," Rudy said. His head nodded up and down, and he was unable to stop it.

Angel thought his bat-like ears looked like he was about to fly away.

"What if," Rudy said, "you were just a pretty face until one day the groomer accidentally shocked you with a bad hair dryer? And that created Underdog Cat?"

Giggling, Angel said, "No!"

"What if you were just a pretty face until one day, your translator shocked you?"

"No! Stop with the electric shocks. That's no fun."

"But Spiderman gets bit by a radioactive spider. You want something like that?"

"No! It has to be right for a cat. Something about Kittywood."

Rudy stopped to climb onto a park bench. Standing on his hind legs, he boomed like a tour guide and said, "Kittywood is built in a forgotten valley, somewhere in the United States. Its location is a carefully guarded secret. Tourists are only allowed to visit if they ride in special passenger helicopters with no windows. While digging the foundation for Majestic Kennels, they unearthed a strange rock."

Nodding eagerly, Angel said, "Why was Kittywood's valley forgotten? Why had no one lived there for centuries? Perhaps—yes—aliens, or an ancient civilization, once lived in this valley. They left things—maybe magical rocks—that protected the valley."

Eyes glowing, Rudy's voice deepened. "The strange rock was large, and it shimmered like a rainbow, sometimes golden, sometimes rosy, and sometimes bluish. It was magical. Obviously."

"It could've ended up in a museum, but no one wanted it taken far away. So Grace and Albert Persian bought the Shimmer Rock," Angel said.

Nodding, Rudy jumped down, almost stumbling before catching himself. "The Shimmer Rock is displayed in the Persians' penthouse apartment. Some wonder if it's the real reason the Persians have had such an amazing KittyTube career."

"Of course not! MamaGrace and DaddyAlbert work hard!"

Rudy flicked his large ears. "I know they do and so does everyone else. This is just the Underdog Cat story. So, as I was saying, the magical Shimmer Rock was the first thing that Angel Persian saw when she opened her eyes."

"No," Angel said. "It wasn't."

"Stop arguing with me! This is the Underdog Cat story, so of course, it's not real."

This isn't the truth, Angel told herself. *It's just my Underdog Cat mythology. Doesn't matter if the facts get changed.*

"Anyway," Rudy said, "the first thing that Angel Persian saw when her eyes opened at ten days old—"

"Actually, they opened at eleven days old." Angel held up a paw. "Oh, sorry."

Rudy rolled his eyes.

Excitement tingled through Angel from nose to tail. This was good storytelling!

Rudy continued, "The first thing Angel Persian saw when her eyes opened at ten days old was the Shimmer Rock. It blinded her, changed her, so that she closed her eyes. The next day, at eleven days old"—Rudy shook a paw at Angel—"she opened them again and did her eye-opening video."

"The Shimmer Rock bestowed powers to the kitten, making her Underdog Cat," Angel said slowly. "The Shimmer Rock was set in this valley to protect it. And now, Underdog Cat was given the ability—and the responsibility—to protect Kittywood."

Angel and Rudy stared at each other, eyes wide and round.

"Wow," Rudy said. "You're Underdog Cat, the protector of Kittywood."

Malachi-Glenys Kennels–Green Screen

Angel stepped into the Malachi-Glenys Kennels, glad to be out of the glaring sun. It was early fall, but the day felt like high summer, hot and humid. Malachi-Glenys was a sprawling series of buildings. Each one had tall columns and a soaring roof, with an open feel that startled Angel. She was used to Majestic Kennels' small studios cluttered with lights and cameras.

Here, the studios disappeared into black ceilings. Cavernous, they echoed strangely.

When she mentioned the echoes, a camera operator said, "We know how to use our microphones to prevent any echoes."

"Of course," Angel said. "I didn't mean to criticize." She spun around the open space, entranced but unsteady.

The door flung back, and Director Esha swept in. From a distance, she was a rich red color. But up close, her eyes looked like they'd been outlined with white eyeliner. It was just lines of white fur, but the effect was striking. "Get that green screen set up," she called.

Behind her, a crew of men pushed wheelbarrows to the stage and dumped sand in piles. Other men raked the sand into a level surface while Angel watched, bewildered. Still other men carried in green screens to set up at the back of the stage.

"Angel, over here," said Director Esha.

Angel dodged the men and stepped offstage to talk to the director.

"What I want today is a beach scene," said Director Esha. "People are worried about the coming winter and want a distraction. Malachi-Glenys concentrates on seasonal videos. Our beach videos peak in popularity in late fall."

Angel nodded, but her heart did flip-flops. Green screen technology meant they would add a digital background. She'd perform in the studio, but they'd use the computer to add a beach background. It would look like they'd flown to a beach to videotape.

"Are you listening?" Director Esha snapped.

"Um, yes. It's just that Majestic Kennels never does green screen."

Director Esha rolled her eyes, her whiskers quivering. "Sometimes Director Stanley is old-fashioned. It makes perfect sense to use green screen technology. We can't fly to a beach for a video."

For a moment, Angel let herself wish. A beach. Would the sea breeze smell like fish all day? That sounded heavenly. Then she shook herself and concentrated. "What do you want me to do?"

"Acrobatics."

Angel sighed. "I was hoping to do more Underdog Cat videos. I've been working on the story behind the character. If you have time, I could tell you—"

"No." Director Esha looked over Angel's head and yelled, "Smoother! And get that palm tree set up." Turning back, she shook her head at Angel. "I don't want Underdog Cat. You're doing well with acrobatics. You'll climb the palm tree and do a flip off of it. It'll look like you land in the water, and we'll add a big splash."

Angel frowned. "Like a water cat?"

"No, dear. Like a beach cat."

Swallowing hard, Angel said, "Sounds great." This wasn't going the way she had expected. After working with Rudy, she'd hoped to get the director behind the Underdog Cat idea. Instead, she was going to do some strange beach thing. Shuddering, she wondered how that sand would feel on her feet. Would it get in her fur?

"Um, who's my groomer today? I'll just get my grooming session started while they finish setting up."

"Oh." Director Esha looked Angel over, up, and down. "Hold out your foot."

Angel extended a paw.

"You look fine to me." Director Esha shrugged. "I only use a groomer once a week. I know Director Stanley spoils the kittens with groomers, but you won't get that here at Malachi-Glenys. If you want a groomer, you must let us know the day before. And I may not approve it, anyway. We like the natural look here."

"But my fur is different. It needs—"

A man approached the director and said, "It's done."

"Great. Angel, walk around the set and get used to the feel of the sand."

Bewildered, Angel turned toward the light. She tiptoed onto the sand, grimacing at the gritty feel.

"Try climbing the palm tree," called Director Esha.

Soft cardboard covered the fake tree. Angel stretched high to dig in her claws, then pull her hindquarters up. She stretched and pulled several more times to reach the top. Taking a deep breath, she hid in the leaves for a minute to look out over the studio.

It was so different from Majestic Kennels' studios.

The set only took up half of the studio space. Bright lights flooded the sand, making it sparkle, like it might shine on a real beach. But the sand and green screen looked ridiculous on this set. They might get a good video from this, but it was so, well, so fake.

"Try a flip from the tree," called Director Esha.

Angel inched toward the edge of the palm branch. It was higher than she liked. When she'd learned acrobatics from Captain Piper, they'd usually only stacked cubes about three cubes high, or about nine feet. This was maybe twelve feet. She hadn't liked the four-cube-high stacks, though she could do it.

"Angel, the flip—can you try it now?" called Director Esha.

With a deep breath, Angel leaped, controlling her spin. Head over, legs over, look for the ground. Plop! She landed badly on the sand. It wasn't as soft as the cushioned mat that she usually used. She wavered a moment, then took a step, testing her legs. The sand squished into her paw fur, so Angel lifted a front paw and shook it. She shook the other paw, but that meant she had to put the clean paw into the sand again.

Oh, she hated sand.

"Fantastic," called Director Esha. "That looked amazing. Let's practice two more times and then we'll turn on the cameras. Next time, see if you can stretch out a little more and land farther away from the tree."

Angel sighed. This was going to be a long, hot day at the beach.

Director Esha

The next week, Angel sat outside Director Esha's door. Waiting. Over thirty minutes already. She'd been told to come and talk to the director about the beach video. It hadn't done well. But what was there to talk about? Instead, she hoped to explain the Underdog Cat ideas.

Comfortable, colorful pillows lined one wall for cats, while chairs for humans lined another wall. By now, though, Angel was pacing.

"Much longer?" Angel asked the human receptionist, Miss Vanessa. Her hair color was almost the same red-gold as Director Esha's fur. Angel wondered if that was on purpose.

"You can't rush her," Miss Vanessa said. "She's still listening to the new sound recordings."

Wade Abyssinian, Director Esha's husband, was famous for his sound recordings done "in the wild." He might record the sound of a boat bumping against a dock, or a fountain splashing. Once, he recorded a beehive, and it became the background sound for a summer video of cats walking in a flower meadow. The video ranked well, and comments always mentioned the beehive sounds. Interesting soundtracks were part of Malachi-Glenys's unique videos.

The door slammed open. "Angel!" called Director Esha.

Squawking birds called from the director's office.

Angel turned, uncertain.

"Listen to this! Wade's just come back from a trip to a zoo. He recorded some parrots. What do you think? Would it work with your beach video? We could digitally add a parrot flying across the video."

Angel edged into the large office. The walls were covered with paintings of birds. From elaborate to simple frames, from gigantic to small, the paintings were a wild splash of color making the room a jungle of birds.

Eyes wide, Angel looked from the director to Mr. Wade. The Abyssinians were both the same color. Wade was slightly larger, but otherwise, they almost looked like twins. They stood confidently—

Of course they're confident, Angel told herself. *They run this kennel.* It was just SO different from Majestic Kennels and Director Stanley.

"Um." Angel tried to imagine the video with a parrot.

"Yes!" Director Esha said. "I'm glad you agree. We'll get editing on it right away. And we'll rerelease the video. It was only number nineteen for the week. But we do this often, reedit the film and release it again. Tweak it. We usually get some lift in rankings. Maybe it'll go up to twelve or thirteen."

Angel blinked. She had no idea that they could even DO that. Did Majestic Kennels ever rerelease a video?

"Now, was there anything else?"

Mind blank, Angel just stared.

Director Esha tapped on the recorder to turn off the parrot song. "If not…"

"Oh, yes," Angel said. "I wanted to explain the back story for Underdog Cat. It's been a great role for me, and—"

Director Esha shook her head and shoved to her feet. "We've already discussed that. We'll do an Underdog Cat video, but not all that nonsense about an origin story. If that's all, I have to get to a videotaping." She swept past Angel into the reception area. "Vanessa, get us a reservation at the Gledhill Fish Company for lunch."

She glanced back at Angel. "I'll see you at 1:00 p.m. sharp in Studio 3B."

Angel's heart sank. Her time at Malachi-Glenys wasn't going as she had hoped. She still had to keep her views as high as possible, but working with this Director was like being run over by a train.

Director Esha moved fast and decisively but didn't listen to anything Angel said.

Angel knew one thing for sure: Malachi-Glenys wasn't a studio where she would feel at home. What if her only contract offer was from them?

EPISODE 5

Underdog Cat to the Rescue

Standing on the top of Majestic Kennels, Underdog Cat watches children drifting out of the school building. Yes, many human children live in Kittywood—the sons and daughters of chefs, doctors, groomers, elevator operators, camera operators, film editors, and accountants. The city leaders built a school for the children, so the parents bring their families to live and work here.

It's a good place to live—except right now, there's construction.

The city is building a new library and needs to widen one of the streets near the school.

Walking home, children head in that direction.

DETOUR! ROAD CLOSED!

Some children hesitate, confused. But the sign points them toward the other corner, the corner without a traffic light.

The afternoon wind ruffles Underdog Cat's pure white fur.

Eeee!

The sound jerks her head around. That was tires squealing!

She searches the city, looking for the car that made that sound.

There, near the school. The detour sign has confused a car driver, too.

Squeal! The car swerves.

Look out! You almost hit that kid!

Never fear! Underdog Cat is here!

Underdog Cat swoops down to the street. She strides into the intersection and holds up a hand.

STOP!

Cars slow, stop.

Underdog Cat motions for the kids. Come. Cross now.

Kids stream across the road.

A car inches forward, but Underdog Cat stands firm.

STOP!

The kids are across.

Underdog Cat skips to the sidewalk. She motions for traffic to continue.

Then one last child appears. She's small but carries a heavy backpack. Staring up at Underdog Cat, she says, "Will you help me?"

Underdog Cat nods. She watches for a break in traffic. When the cars have passed, she escorts the child across.

The girl turns to thank her.

But Underdog Cat shakes her head as if to say, "No. I'll walk with you. I won't leave you till you're safely home."

Together, they stroll down the sidewalk.

Underdog Cat saves the day.

Again.

TALK IT OUT

Director Domingo

"Why are you letting them say no to the Underdog Cat origin stories?" Rudy asked. "You have clout. The 'Underdog Cat to the Rescue' video is doing well. Go back and bargain."

Angel shook her head. The morning was cool and overcast. The weather forecast called for rain later, so she was glad to be out early with Rudy.

"Director Esha knows what she wants. She won't listen."

Rudy's voice deepened. "You're acting like you're a nobody. But you're one of the top kittens."

Everything at Malachi-Glenys was different, though. She said, "Will we ever stop worrying about our acting?"

Rudy's head nodded rhythmically, like he was keeping the beat for some unheard music. "No," he said. "We just have to trust the directors."

"Good morning!"

The kittens whirled to see Director Domingo running toward them. He stopped and said, "Angel, have you seen the rankings this morning on your slo-mo acrobatics videos?"

Angel shook her head. She hadn't stopped by the leaderboard yet. The video's editing had been fantastic, much better than she'd expected.

"The video is holding in the top ten for the third week in a row. That's amazing."

Angel cocked her head, her brow furrowed. "Your kennel did amazing work on it." It was always a good thing to give credit to someone else.

Director Domingo sat and lifted his back leg to scratch behind his ear. He licked the fur on his right front foot. "Are you interested in doing more acrobatics videos? Are you learning any new tricks?"

Angel's eyes widened. He wanted her to do more videos with Wells Brothers. He was asking if she wanted to work with them. A contract from Wells Brothers? Would she be happy there?

Director Domingo's green eyes studied her, waiting for an answer.

Stammering, Angel said, "Um. Yes, of course. I just want to work. But I've tried new tricks with Captain Piper, and it's hard for a cat body to do twists and more complicated things."

The large Manx cat stared a moment longer and then shook his head slightly. "So acrobatics isn't your thing?"

"Yes, oh, yes! I love it. It's just that—"

Director Domingo waited.

"—well, I like the Underdog Cat role, too."

"Hmmm. I think you've outgrown that one. Your brother, Quincy, is still doing well with his food videos. He may never outgrow that." Director Domingo shook out his fur. "Well, I've got to finish my run. We'll talk again later." He charged off, scampering down the sidewalk.

Rudy head-butted Angel's side. "Director Domingo likes you!"

"Maybe."

But I blew it, Angel thought. *He could tell that I wasn't excited about the acrobatics.*

Without thinking, she started jogging along the sidewalk, watching the director disappear in the distance.

Angel's thoughts were jumbled. She loved acrobatics but she didn't see them as a long-term solution because cats couldn't do the more complicated moves. Where was the future in that? She loved the Underdog Cat too. Maybe it would have more staying power if they'd just listen to the back story she and Rudy had created.

"Angel!"

She spun around. Rudy was leaning over, panting. She'd been running and not thinking about him and his illness. And he'd tried to keep up with her.

She raced back to him. "Are you okay?"

Rudy let his body sink to the ground and curled up. "Oh, that was too much. I need to be more careful."

"Rudy." Angel tried not to say it. But it had to be said. "You have to talk to Director Stanley."

"No!" Rudy pushed up and stood unsteadily for a moment.

He glared, then marched stiffly back to the kennel. "No!" He whirled around. "No!"

"Okay. Okay." Rudy tottered along. Angel's heart ached for her small friend. He was working hard to get a contract, but would he be able to keep acting? Was there nothing the doctors could do? She licked her lips, her mouth suddenly dry.

Should she tell Director Stanley?

Cardinal Kennels

The next week, Angel and Rudy were assigned to Cardinal Kennels. Like Malachi-Glenys, it wasn't a single building. Instead, a fenced area held about a dozen buildings, from vast warehouses to four-story offices to tiny huts for the guards.

After visiting other kennels, Angel had realized that Majestic Kennels was odd to house everything in one building.

Rudy reported to Studio 1, one of the warehouse building, for an early filming. Angel, though, was directed to the kennel offices. She wouldn't be on set until later that day.

"Angel! I'm glad to work with you this week." Director Raquel motioned for Angel to come into her office. "How's your mother? Is Albert's 'Puss and Boots' film doing well?"

The sleek black cat had visited the Persian family a couple of times. Angel didn't remember much except Director Raquel's smooth voice. "Now, tell me about your acting. You've done some acrobatics, and there's the Underdog Cat character."

Eagerly, Angel shared her ideas for the Underdog Cat back story. Finally someone was taking the time to listen!

"I love the idea! A Shimmer Rock sounds fabulous." Director Raquel rose to pace the room.

Plush rugs filled the floor, giving it an exotic look. Angel loved how it felt under her paws.

Director Raquel stopped to peer out the window.

Angel's spirits lifted. Curly had been enthusiastic about Cardinal Kennel. Just having someone listen to her ideas gave Angel hope. Maybe…

Director Raquel came back to sit in front of Angel, settling her chin on her paws. "It's interesting. But it has lots of problems."

Angel shook her head. "Like what?"

"It needs too many special effects. The Shimmer Rock, for example. How would you make it shimmer? No, it's not really a Kittywood video. Hollywood is the place for special effects, not Kittywood. Our specialty is being cute cats. Not doing special effects. When we try it, our videos just look silly."

Angel's stomach cramped with disappointment. She drew a deep breath, trying to think how to convince the director. "Well—"

"I think Underdog Cat is a great role, and we're planning a couple videos. But the backstory just doesn't work."

"I could show you a script—"

A knock at the door interrupted them.

Director Raquel shook her head. "Instead, I have a surprise for you."

The office door opened. There stood DaddyAlbert, tall and handsome. His black, red and gold fur was casually rumpled, a look that took a groomer a long time to achieve. Behind him, another cat pushed forward, and Angel recognized him as Magnus Bombay, Director Raquel's husband. His eyes gleamed like gold nuggets inside his inky face.

"For your first Cardinal Kennels video, you're going to rescue your father."

Angel just stared. Rescue her father? What?

"Here's the thing, Angel," Director Raquel said, "Albert Persian will get views."

Angel nodded dumbly.

"And if he's in your video, that means you'll get more views. It's good for everyone."

Stuttering, Angel said, "I-i-is that f-f-fair?"

DaddyAlbert laughed. "Of course it's fair!"

"That's Kittywood!" Director Raquel waved her paw toward her husband, Magnus. "We reached out and suggested it. Of course, your daddy said yes. Anything to help his children succeed, he said."

Angel shrank back, embarrassed. *Maybe,* she thought, *my acting is bad. Director Stanley worked with me a lot, but I don't know if I'm any good. Maybe, I need DaddyAlbert's help. Maybe I can't get views without the family name and reputation.*

"Best of all, we'll work together." DaddyAlbert's green eyes glittered. "We've never done that before."

Anger flushed through her, and Angel stood stiffly. They expected her to be happy. Instead, intense heat throbbed through her. The Underdog Cat story was good. Good! And Kittywood could do it. Easily. She didn't need the Golden One to save her career. She was doing fine on her own, thank you very much.

But...

This was her last month as a kitten.

Tears stung her eyes. It was her worst fear: she wasn't a good actor. She had to have help from her father to even get a contract.

But she needed a contract from Majestic Kennels. Or somewhere.

Swallowing hard, she nuzzled DaddyAlbert's nose. She whispered, "Thanks."

"That's my girl," DaddyAlbert said. "You know, Angel, this is just how things get done in Kittywood."

EPISODE 6

The Rescue of Albert Persian

Albert Persian strolls the sidewalk of downtown Kittywood. He bows to this cat and stops to chat with that one. The Golden One enjoys his evening ramble.

Above, high atop Majestic Kennels, Underdog Cat watches her city. She waits, ready to help when needed.

Wait. Albert isn't watching where he's walking.

There's a construction zone near the school. Today they've dug deep holes for foundations. Danger alert!

Albert turns to look across the street. He waves a paw at a distant cat. He walks straight for a deep hole.

Look out!

Too late. He's fallen. His body lies still.

Is he—?

No, his tail twitches.

He's alive!

Never fear!

Underdog Cat is here!

She leaps into action! She swoops down to the construction zone. Carefully, she scoots around a DANGER sign.

The hole is deep, and Albert is large.

Can she pick him up and fly him out of the hole?

No.

Quick-witted, Underdog Cat sees a ladder. Awkward, she hooks a paw over the top rung. She heaves it to the hole, step by step, and lowers it to Albert. She leaps into the hole.

How strong is Underdog Cat?

Strong enough!

She heaves Albert onto her shoulders.

She staggers up the ladder, one step, next step, yet another weary step.

Be strong. One more step.

Finally she rolls Albert to the ground.

By now, an ambulance has arrived. Quickly, the emergency responders load Albert onto a stretcher. The ambulance roars off into the night, its siren wailing. Wee-wah! Wee-wah!

But Underdog Cat still has work to do. Someone else might fall into that hole, so she must protect her city.

Looking around, she sees orange plastic safety fencing. She grabs iron rods and jams them into the ground around the hole. She attaches the orange fencing to the rods. There. No one else will fall into it.

Underdog Cat saves the day. Again.

Fox Kennels, Great Ideas!

JUST KITTEN AROUND Joke

Q: Why do cats make terrible storytellers?

A: They only have one tail!

"Here at Fox Kennels, we have great ideas!" said Director Ginger. Despite being a tiny Singapura cat, she seemed to fill the room. Her tail twitched, her whiskers quivered, and her paws were always in motion, gesturing this way or that. "We've been planning for you, Angel Persian."

"I'm thrilled," Angel said, and meant it. After the roller coaster of Cardinal Kennels, she just wanted someone to tell her what to do. Her hopes had been raised when Director Raquel listened so carefully to the Underdog Cat story. And her hopes had been dashed when the director swept it all away with the objection about special effects. Working with DaddyAlbert had been amazing, and the video was climbing the charts. Definitely a good thing. But other kittens had been taunting her about "getting Daddy's help."

Fox Kennels, she hoped, would be a better experience.

"Are you ready for this?" Director Ginger asked. The director's office was a penthouse at the top of Fox Kennels. The Fox Kennels building was only five stories tall, about half the height of Majestic Kennels, the highest building in the city. But Fox Kennels had magnificent views of the city center.

Angel nodded and leaned forward. She felt awful. Her hair hadn't been groomed a single time last week at Cardinal Kennels, and a knot was forming under her left front leg. She needed to see a groomer today, even if she had to pay for it.

"Even though Grace Persian hasn't appeared in a video in a couple of years, Grace and Albert still dominate KittyTube. Their classic videos still do well. To satisfy fans, we need a tour of their penthouse apartment. We're working on a documentary with a Hollywood film studio."

Angel wanted to groan, to protest, to say no.

Not her family again. She wanted to be successful on her own, not because of her family.

"And we want you," said Director Ginger with a sweep of her paws, "to be our tour guide. Isn't that a great idea?"

Angel said nothing.

"We've already gotten permission. Grace will meet you there at 8:00 a.m.—"

"No," Angel said. She was suddenly very tired of being told what to do. "No. You need to schedule me with a groomer at 8:00 a.m. Then I'll meet MamaGrace at 10:00 a.m. for the filming."

Director Ginger fell back, eyes wide. Then she walked around Angel, studying her fur.

Angel tried to turn to watch the director, so they spun around a couple of times, like humans dancing a waltz together.

"Ah, you were at the Cardinal Kennels last week?"

Angel nodded.

"Raquel Bombay is a fool. She barely needs a groomer, so she doesn't understand someone like you. With that long white fur—you must be very uncomfortable."

Angel nodded, looking down at herself. Her paws were dingy with dust. The mirror told her this morning that her eyes were crusty. And that underarm knot hurt.

Director Ginger asked, "Is there a groomer you prefer?"

"Oh, yes! Miss Tanya knows my hair and how to do it the best."

"All right. You have an appointment with Miss Tanya at 8:00 a.m. Be at the Persian penthouse at 10:00 a.m."

Walking out of Fox Kennels, Angel realized that the grooming had completely taken over the conversation. She had no idea what they wanted her to do when they toured the penthouse. Was she supposed to point out interesting things? Would they have a human narrator or just add text to the video?

But it was hard to be upset.

Tomorrow she'd see Miss Tanya!

EPISODE 7

Angel Persian's Tour of the Persian Penthouse

CUE

Music. It's a popular Ivory Bongo Harp Band song.

Angel knocks on the penthouse door.

It opens, and there is MamaGrace.

Not that you can see her. Light streams into the room from the huge floor-to-ceiling windows. That creates backlighting that leaves MamaGrace as a dark shadow, nothing more. She's agreed to the penthouse tour, but only if they don't show her face or record her limping.

MamaGrace gestures a welcome.

Angel strides into the room. Looking back, she does a soul-connect with the camera, her odd-colored eyes gleaming. It's intimate, saying, "Come and see my childhood home."

The open room is spare and simple. A few scattered cushions. Mostly, the penthouse is about the windows. Angel leaps lightly onto the wide windowsill and sits looking out over the city. Her tail hangs off the sill and twitches.

The camera scans over her head and looks out over the city too.

It's a spectacular view, high enough to give a drone's-eye perspective. There's Malachi-Glenys Kennels with its columned buildings. And Fox Kennels, the second-highest building in the city. The school for the human children. And the tall waterfront building that holds the Doodle Studio, full of Miss Doodle's amazing costumes.

Beautiful. Peaceful. An amazing city made possible by the success of KittyTube.

And its most successful stars are Grace and Albert Persian.

Angel rises gracefully and pads silently to the next room. A low dining table with stools fills the room, a place of happy family meals. Angel sits in her seat and gestures toward each of the other chairs.

Text: Albert sits at one end of the table.

Text: Mama Grace sits at the other end.

Text: Quincy, Angel's brother, sits on the left side, opposite Angel.

Text: PittyPat, Angel's sister, sits on the right side beside Angel.

Her heart is full of memories: DaddyAlbert singing to MamaGrace, PittyPat talking and talking, Quincy eating and eating. She shakes away the happy memories. She cannot cry. Not on camera.

Next, the camera follows Angel to each of the bedrooms. There's a larger one for Angel and PittyPat. Angel is surprised at how small the room looks. *I've grown*, she thinks. In Angel's mind, PittyPat's voice echoes through the room, making Angel ache to visit her sister.

Multicolored sleeping cushions fill the floor of Quincy's room. An erratic sleeper, Quincy always wandered, sleeping on one cushion for an hour and then switching to another. Angel wonders if he still does that. She gulps at a sudden wave of longing for her brother.

Finally the camera follows Angel into Grace and Albert Persian's bedroom. A large red silk cushion sits beside the window. Angel remembers the early days, when DaddyAlbert was stuck in France. Several nights, Angel had crept in to snuggle with MamaGrace while she cried in her sleep.

Angel pats a gigantic sleeping cushion. There are two indentations, side by side, where the Persians sleep. Joy fills Angel, happiness that her father had

found his way home, that MamaGrace is content with life again.

Angel steps onto the windowsill. This room looks east, toward a forest that fills the valley beyond the city. A soothing, beautiful landscape.

Twirling, Angel strides quickly back to the public rooms and sweeps a paw around. This, she seems to say, is the Persian family home.

The Leaderboard

Angel stared at the red letters of the leaderboard.

Angel Persian, "Penthouse Tour" was number fifteen.

Ivory Bongo Harp Band ranked number nine with "Concert in the Park."

Jazz Siamese's "Snowman" topped out at number two.

Underdog Cat, with a cameo from Albert Persian, "The Rescue of Albert Persian," hit number one. Number one! Why didn't she feel more excited?

Shaking her head, Angel trudged to the doorway of Majestic Kennels. As she expected, Rudy was there. With the fall season upon them, the sun rose later and later, so it was still dark outside.

"How are you today?" she asked her friend.

"I feel great!" Rudy said. He walked steadily, but watching him, Angel could tell he was already tired.

She remembered the first time she had noticed Rudy, back when Jazz brought him home like a lonely stray. She hadn't liked that he was butting in on her friendship with Jazz. Since then, though, Rudy had changed her in good ways. She could talk to him about her successes and failures. She had learned to listen to him and trust his ideas. He'd become a friend—and that surprised her.

As a friend, she wanted to tell him again that he needed to talk to the Director. She should insist on it. But it might ruin their friendship. Still, friends did the hard things when needed.

"Hey! Can I join you two?"

Startled, Angel shook her head in surprise. PittyPat didn't like to get up early. What was going on?

PittyPat trotted to catch up. "Did you stop by the leaderboard?"

Angel nodded guiltily. She hadn't noticed PittyPat's ranking.

"I'm number four, with my volleyball water sports video!" PittyPat held out a paw for Angel to high-five. "I love Fox Kennels. Director Ginger has so much energy."

Angel sucked in a breath. "Have you talked about a contract?"

Eyes glowing, PittyPat nodded. "Yes!"

Rudy and Angel leaped onto PittyPat, knocking her over, and they rolled in the Catnip Meadow. Rudy shoved away after just a moment, but the sisters wrestled in joy.

Finally they sat up and snuggled.

"Can you believe it?"

"Great job!" Angel said. "Do you remember when we first started dreaming of being stars? You've made a name for yourself with water."

"Thanks." PittyPat ducked her head. "I'm so happy."

Angel thought about the changes coming. The kittens' dorm would empty out one way or another, with kittens moving to new kennels or moving out for other jobs. Where would she go? Fox, Malachi-Glenys, Wells Brothers, Cardinal—she'd tried them all. Nothing felt like home except Majestic. Honestly, though, Majestic was likely to offer contracts to Jazz and to the Ivory Bongo Harp Band. That left her out in the cold. Wells Brothers had been interested in her acrobatics videos. Fox wanted her as a tour guide for the most famous KittyTubers. But nothing felt right.

Turning away from PittyPat, she saw Rudy curled up in the catnip, asleep.

Oh! He was sicker than he knew.

Gently, she patted a paw on his back.

With a start, his eyes popped open, black orbs in his dark face. "Just a power nap!" he said immediately.

Angel's heart twisted in sympathy. "Yes, power naps are great." Tears filled her eyes, but she refused to say anything else.

But PittyPat said, "Rudy, are you feeling all right? You seem slow lately."

At Rudy's glare, Angel shook her head. No, she hadn't told PittyPat about the Devon Rex myopathy.

PittyPat let her hind legs sink into the catnip, but she kept her front legs stiff and straight, looking like a lion statue outside a library. "What's going on with you two? You should both have contract offers by now. This is the last week of touring the kennels."

Angel and Rudy shrugged at each other. They'd talked of little else this month.

"Well," Angel said. "Fox Kennels has talked to me about a contract. They love 'Penthouse Tour.' We'd be together, PittyPat."

PittyPat stomped the catnip. "But do you like it? It doesn't feel right to me. It might bring you fame, but being on KittyTube isn't the only way to happiness. What will make you happy, Angel?" She turned to Rudy. "What will make you happy, Rudy? Do you want a contract with Majestic or a different kennel? Is the band making you happy?"

Angel said slowly, "My only other choices are acrobatics videos, which everyone seems to love, but I don't think they will last. Or the Underdog Cat videos, which no one will let me develop. I haven't found a home yet."

Rudy said, "We've talked and talked about this. I just want the band to get a contract. I'd be happy doing background music—like we did for Angel's 'Penthouse Tours' video. But..."

He was silent, his head wagging up and down.

Almost in tears, Angel said, "Rudy. You have to." Her chest felt like it was going to burst.

PittyPat said, "What?"

"Rudy," Angel said.

"I know," Rudy said.

"What?" PittyPat said. "What?"

Rudy turned to stare into Angel's eyes. "I'll do it now, before breakfast. If you'll do something too."

Angel's tears spilled over.

Rudy said, "You need to make a decision today, too. Will you accept contracts that will make you unhappy?"

Hanging her head, Angel whispered, "I know."

He turned and trudged back to Majestic Kennels.

PittyPat nudged Angel. "What's going on with Rudy?"

Angel buried her face in her sister's fur, drinking in the warmth and strength. She just shook her head and cried for her tiny friend and his courage. And for her own lack of courage.

TALK IT OUT

Rudy and Director Stanley

"I have Devon Rex myopathy."

Director Stanley studied the tiny kitten. "Yowza! Like your uncle Eli?"

Rudy shuddered and nodded. He blinked, clamping down on his emotions. It was so sad to visit Uncle Eli, to watch him choke on his food and limp around. He had to keep a clear head.

The room smelled like peppermint candies. The television screens behind the director ran silent, a reminder that there was an audience of people hungry for a new cat video.

"What do you want to do?" Director Stanley's voice was gruff but gentle.

"Please, sir." Rudy's eyes were wide with hope. "Don't shut me out. The Ivory Bongo Harp Band is a new concept for KittyTube. It deserves a chance, especially here at Majestic. I can keep doing videos for a while. Later, if the illness gets too bad, just replace me, but give Maria and Curly a chance. None of us would get a solo contract but as a band, we're special, different."

The older cat started to shake his head, but Rudy bounded up.

He winced and had to straighten his front legs. "Wait," Rudy said. "Listen."

Director Stanley stilled and motioned a paw that he was listening.

"I have lots of cousins who could fill in for me. Cameos. If I feel bad someday, I could take a day off. If it gets as bad as Uncle Eli's, I'll retire. But then," he continued, his face screwed up, "...could I ...could I write music for the band? I love that as much as playing, actually. I'd be happy as a composer, but to be a composer, I need a band."

"Composer?" Director Stanley tilted his head. "We've never had a cat composer. KittyTube just licenses human music. Or we've done silent videos."

"They used our band's music in Angel's 'Penthouse Tour' video. Did you see it? The music made it truly a KittyTube video. We don't need the humans' music every time now."

Director Stanley looked Rudy over, wincing at the stiff front legs. He shook his head, but said, "Yowza! Very interesting."

Best Friends Forever

Contract Day dawned bright and cool. Kittens gathered early, no one sleeping late, filling the hallway with nervous meows and chitters.

Jazz and Angel woke early too, itching to join the excitement. But at the door, they paused, stared at each other, and almost cried. Angel gulped at the memory of asking Jazz to be her roommate. Jazz had worried because Angel's parents were so popular on KittyTube.

As roommates, they'd talked shop, helped each other with decisions on costumes and episodes, and learned to trust each other.

I was right, Angel thought. *We've become friends.*

But this was the end.

Today was Contract Day. They would meet at 10:00 a.m. in the Wiles Theater in Malachi Glenys Kennels.

By the end of next week, the kittens' dorm would be empty. Jazz was looking at apartments in the upper floors of Majestic Kennels, assuming that she'd be offered a Majestic contract. Angel had seen a couple she liked, but…

...she had no contract offers. Not that she knew about, anyway.

Angel shivered from head to tail-tip, muscles tight with worry. What would she do if she didn't get a contract?

"Do you want to eat breakfast?" Jazz asked.

"No. Maybe after."

"Let's get out of here, then." Jazz's fur stood up, as if ready for a fight. "We can stop in the Catnip Meadow or just stroll the streets or something."

They bustled through the hallway, waving at other kittens, but not stopping to talk. The elevator was too slow for such a day, so they pounded down the stairs and burst out of Majestic Kennels doorway into the open air.

Angel breathed deeply and raced to the Catnip Meadow. She stood in the dew-soaked catnip and closed her eyes against the sun that spilled over the horizon. *Breathe*, she told herself. *Just live this moment.*

Beside her, Jazz said, "Everything changes today. Thanks for being a friend."

Angel turned and pounced! They rolled in friendly battle until, exhausted and wet, they curled and faced east as the pink clouds faded to white with the sunrise.

Today, their future would be decided.

Top Ten-Contract Day

She'd worked hard to be a good actor. And it might not be enough. Angel started licking her fur, grooming it for the 10:00 contract meeting.

Jazz and Angel dallied. They strolled around Catnip Meadow, then dashed toward the humans' school to check on the library construction—almost done! Quickly, they trotted past each kennel, talking about their experiences there.

But in the end, they wound up at Malachi-Glenys Kennels at 9:30 a.m. and walked into the side doors of Wiles Theater. The kitten terraces near the front were packed. This was an event that no one wanted to miss. Jazz and Angel wove through the cats to their place on the front row.

Looking around, Angel's heart thumped. This was it.

From the moment she'd opened her eyes at eleven days old, this is what Angel had been shooting for: to become an actor.

Today, ten lucky kittens would receive contracts to become KittyTube stars. Maybe—if Rudy had been persuasive enough—one of those slots would go to a band, a group of kittens, for the first time ever.

It was a day of possibilities.

So why was Angel so worried?

Because no one had actively recruited her, except Fox Kennels. And she'd told Director Ginger that she couldn't just do tour videos. If they didn't want her for the Underdog Cat videos, then it wasn't a good fit. Director Ginger hadn't liked that, so Fox was probably out.

Angel had good videos, but did she fit into any studio's creative program? Majestic was her home, really. Her only home. But Jazz and Rudy had those slots. Cardinal's video of Underdog Cat only worked because of DaddyAlbert's cameo. How could she work with Malachi-Glenys when Director Esha wouldn't provide her with a groomer? She loved how Wells Brothers edited her acrobatics videos, but she didn't think that role would give her a career.

Did any kennel have a place for her, a home?

Bright music played as the kittens entered.

Oh, Angel thought, *we come here as kittens, but we'll leave as cats.*

The theater's main doors opened, and humans rushed to find seats where they could take photos and cheer for their favorite cat stars. Meows and chattering humans filled the huge room with a restless energy.

Angel leaned back and studied the ceiling. Arlo Porter Wiles was walking with the three cats. Was that scrawny cat Director Stanley? Maybe that black one was Director Raquel. It must have been hard to start KittyTube. Had they started with three kennels? If so, where had the other two come from? The directors of the five kennels were old. Were they tired of the struggle to stay on top? Wells Brothers enjoyed life. Did Director Stanley? How did KittyTube manage to steal the cat videos away from other platforms? It would be interesting to look into the history of KittyTube. Maybe a documentary on each director?

Arlo Porter Wiles's cat translator had given cats the freedom to do whatever they wanted.

Majestic Kennels interpreted that a different way from the other kennels. Maybe Wells Brothers was right: "Enjoy life! It's too short to worry about fame."

Overhead, the theater lights dimmed, and the crowd quieted. Huge lights illuminated the stage, making it possible to stream the event live on social media.

Angel shook herself back to the moment, heart thumping in her throat.

It was a simple event. Each director climbed the steps to the podium and announced the two cats to whom they were offering contracts.

No speeches, no fanfare, no pomp and circumstance. Just the way it had been done for years and would be done for years to come.

First came Raquel Bombay. "Cardinal Kennels is excited to offer a contract to Daniel Siamese for his amazing work as a water cat."

The audience exploded with chirps, claps, and chirrups.

Jazz swiveled her ears forward in excitement and meowed for her brother. "My mom will be so excited!"

Angel bumped her shoulder and meowed loudly too.

When the applause died down, Director Raquel said, "We love dress-up cats, and no one does it as well as Ismo Bobtail. Welcome, Ismo, to Cardinal Kennels."

Another round of applause and excitement spread through the theater.

Two down, eight to go.

The spotlight caught Director Stanley climbing the stairs.

Angel had heard his voice the night she was born. He'd always been a part of her life, wrinkles and all. Her chest tightened. Her breaths came hard and fast. She knew what was coming—and yet, she hoped she was wrong.

"The most successful kitten this year will join Majestic Kennels!" Director Stanley said. "Yowza! Welcome, Jazz Siamese, as our newest dress-up cat."

Jazz stood, and a spotlight caught her wave to the crowd; across the theater, cameras flashed, fans recording the moment. Across the theater, her brother, Daniel, looked ready to explode with excitement.

Angel looked behind them at the rows of family cats. The Siamese family was hugging and crying. Both of their children had been given contracts, an amazing thing for a family new to Kittywood.

Angel's parents were clapping the Siamese family on the back and congratulating them.

MamaGrace and DaddyAlbert would expect all their children to have contracts today. What if Angel was the one to disappoint them?

Director Stanley held up a paw for silence. "Majestic is also excited about our next contract because it's a new thing for Kittywood. We are offering a contract to a group of kittens who've created a new category of videos, the Ivory Bongo Harp Band. Rudy Devon Rex, Curly Singapura, and Maria Devon Rex, we're thrilled that you'll be joining us this year."

Angel's heart was ready to burst with joy. Rudy had done it! She had started him on his musical career by suggesting he try the piano cat role. But Rudy, Curly, and Maria had taken the band to amazing places.

But her heart also broke. She would never be a Majestic Kennel star.

Emotions dueled in her chest: pride and excitement for her friends, and despair for herself.

Overwhelmed, Angel barely heard Director Esha announce the Malachi-Glenys contracts. First was Blondie Abyssinian, a chase cat who'd been born at the kennel and was coming home. And a new food cat, Alisa British Shorthair.

Angel meowed approval with everyone else. But she was aware that six of the ten had now been chosen. Her chances were narrowing.

Director Domingo lumbered up the stairs and, in his big voice, announced, "Wells Brothers is excited to claim the son of Grace and Albert Persian.

Welcome, Quincy Persian! You're one of the most unique food cats we've worked with in a long time."

Angel whirled around to wave at Quincy, who was grinning from ear to ear. He was going to be so happy at Wells Brothers!

"Our other choice," said Director Domingo, "is Joaquin Maine Coon, a fabulous chase cat."

Angel sucked in a deep breath. So she didn't get Wells Brothers, either.

Finally Ginger Singapura climbed the steps, each step almost too tall for her short frame. She would announce the last two contracts.

Angel shrank into a tight ball. She wasn't going to be chosen. What would she do?

Director Ginger said, "Fox Kennels is very excited to welcome PittyPat Persian as our water cat. She's doing amazing things with water volleyball, and we see a long, happy career for her."

Angel stood to wave both paws at PittyPat and Quincy and her parents. So amazing.

But she shrank back into a tight ball.

"Our last contract," said Director Ginger, "welcomes Aurora Devon Rex as an innocent. And any other small things I can think of!"

A ripple of laughter swept through the theater.

But Angel couldn't breathe.

No contract.

No contract.

No contract.

***

REPORTING LIVE FROM KITTYWOOD – Contract Day

"This is a strange year," one reporter said, "with twelve kittens receiving contracts. The Ivory Bongo Harp Band counts as one contract, but it was for three kittens."

Another focused on the tragedies. "Contract Day leaves some amazing kittens out in the cold. The biggest surprise is that Angel Persian didn't receive a contract. She's done well during her time at the kittens' dorm, but somehow, she didn't pick up support from any kennel."

The reporter stuck a microphone at Angel. "Would you care to comment?"

Angel turned away. Silent. Heartbroken.

***

MamaGrace was there to lead her home to the Persian penthouse, where she hid all afternoon, numb and unable to think or talk. But that evening,

Quincy and PittyPat celebrated. Jazz and Daniel and their family joined the party.

Everyone partied.

Except Angel.

Eventually, she found her way to the penthouse patio. That's where she had started so many Underdog Cat videos, watching the city below.

Kittywood's lights winked at her. *I love this city,* Angel thought.

But the city—the kennels—don't love me.

What was she going to do?

What I Really Want

JUST KITTEN AROUND Joke

Q: What side of a cat has the most fur?

A: The outside!

Behind her, a door opened. Angel twisted her head to see who it was. Director Stanley. The night sky was velvety black, leaving the terrace in a comforting darkness. Angel didn't want the director to see her tears.

She ignored him and paced the patio walls, protected from the edge by sturdy fencing. She stomped the north wall to the west wall, the south wall to the east. When her circle returned her to Director Stanley, he was curled up. Waiting.

Angel hesitated. Rudy was her inspiration. He'd started as an unlikely kitten, small, awkward, and unsure. But the piano cat role had inspired him. He'd gathered a team, and the Ivory Bongo Harp

Band had taken KittyTube by storm. But it was too late for her.

That's what I want, Angel thought. *To be part of something new.*

"Angel, we have to talk. You can't avoid me forever."

With a sigh, she sat beside him. "Yes, sir?"

Softly, he said, "You're probably pretty sad right now."

Angel whirled away. "I don't want to talk about it."

She returned to pace the patio again. But by the time she completed the circuit, she had calmed enough to flop beside him. Startled, she realized that she was just as large as he was. She remembered quivering in his office, a tiny kitten.

"Well?" he asked.

"You know what? I'm glad I didn't get a contract." Surprised, Angel realized it was true.

Director Stanley nodded, his big ears looking like bats against the dark sky.

"All the kennels are great, but they aren't home," she said.

"Where is home?"

Angel gulped. Majestic was home, of course. But this cat hadn't offered her a contract. How could she say that to him?

"Where is home?" he repeated.

Angel shook her head, emotions clogging her throat so that she couldn't speak.

"I'm trying to help," Director Stanley said. "If you could be anywhere, doing anything, what would it be?"

Had anyone ever asked Angel that question?

Without thinking she said, "What I really want is to start with an idea and end with a finished video. I want to be hands-on in every stage of a video."

The thought stunned her.

But then, she thought back to what she'd learned in the last six months. She'd suggested so many video ideas or changes to ideas, such as the cat sleeping during the storm, or Rudy as a piano cat. She'd learned that post-production was important; success meant much more than the initial idea and the development of the story before shooting.

"Yowza!" Director Stanley said. "But what would that look like?"

"In Hollywood, they do production companies," Angel said, trying to work out her ideas and put them into words. "But then, I'd need someone to distribute the videos, to get them to KittyTube."

"That would be something new," Director Stanley said. "It would take a lot of work to get funding, and all the help you'd need."

"I think I've been training all my life to do something like this," she said. "I want to choose scripts, suggest roles, tweak lighting, and so much more. Everything that goes into a great video—I want to do that. For that, I need to be behind the scenes, part of the conversations about all of that. But I also want to be the actor." She paused, looking at the stars and allowing herself to dream. "I think I'd start with the Underdog Cat. I love that role, and KittyTube viewers love it. I believe in that role."

She trailed off. Because this was all shocking to think about.

Except…she thought of the ceiling in Wiles Theater. Once upon a time, there was no KittyTube. Someone had to start the kennels and KittyTube and all their traditions, and build Kittywood, and… well, why couldn't she do something new? Not a kennel, that was too much for her right now. But… something.

Looking up, she was surprised to see Director Stanley pacing. She watched him make the circuit of the patio: north, west, south, and east.

Finally he stood before her. "I'm old and tired. Soon I'll need someone to take over Majestic Kennels. I thought your father, Albert, might do that, but he's not interested." He hesitated.

"I'll distribute your films. Start your production company, Angel. Write scripts. Act. Produce some great videos. I don't know if you can do it or not. But let's see where it goes. I have lots of friends, and I'll help you get the funding you need. Your parents can help too."

"Oh." A surge of joy shot through her, and she twirled in the night breeze. She was going to start a video production company.

A shaft of light shot across the terrace. Turning, Rudy was silhouetted in the doorway.

He turned around and called, "Hey! The party is out here."

The doors flung wide open and someone turned on the terrace's fairy lights, a magical glow. Everyone came out: Rudy, Jazz, PittyPat, Quincy, Maria, Curly, MamaGrace, DaddyAlbert, and more.

"What's going on?" Rudy demanded.

Director Stanley shrugged at Angel and swept a paw to give her the stage.

"Um," Angel began. But her voice grew stronger as she looked at her friends and family. "I'm going to start a production company. Director Stanley has agreed to distribute any videos that I do. I'll need a team. I'll need help."

Silence.

Then, Rudy said, "I'll write songs for your videos."

Maria said, "The band will do cameos for you."

"I'll do cameos," Jazz, PittyPat, and Quincy said.

DaddyAlbert and MamaGrace nosed Angel and purred, "We knew you'd find a place here in Kittywood. Let us know how we can help."

Angel walked among her friends, celebrating their contracts and her own newfound confidence that she could do something different. Her heart was full of friend and family and possibilities.

Finally Rudy found her, and they drifted to the edge of the terrace. Side by side, they gazed at the brilliant stars twinkling over Kittywood.

Rudy leaned into her shoulder, a warm presence. A friend. "Are you really happy about this? You've tried so many things that weren't quite right. Is a production company a place where you can be at home?"

"Yes! I want this!" Angel said. "Oh, yes!"

And above their heads, a light streaked across the sky, a shooting star. It was a glittering night of destiny.

EPISODE 8

Follow the Kittens

A video by the Angel Production Company

LIGHTS!

A spotlight stabs the dark, revealing the Ivory Bongo Harp Band. Rudy is waiting on the bass keys. Curly hugs her bongos. Maria's claws poise over the harp strings.

CAMERA!

The camera's red light glows.

ACTION!

Curly pounds the bongos, a thrumming beat, while Rudy stalks along the keyboard. Above the melody, the harp strings weave in and out.

While the music continues in the background, the images switch to the landscape of Kittywood.

The bustling marina with boats coming and going.

A restaurant.

Kids laughing and screaming on a playground. Suddenly they stop and rush to greet some cats. Look! It's the Ivory Bongo Harp Band stars.

Rudy, Curly, and Maria prance around the playground and the kids join in for a line dance.

Follow the Kittens

Follow the kittens!
Paws left Right
Paws left Right
Stay right Left
Right Left

Leap high Hide low
Leap high Hide low
Stay low Go high
Low High

Follow the kittens!
Get your tail ready!
Wave it up Down
Wave it up Down
To the left Right
Left Right

Are you ready
for the round and round?
On four! Get ready!
On four, chase your tail:
One
Two
Three

Four

Chase your tail

Chase your tail

Chase

Chase

Chase

Chase!

Stop! AND drop!

Curl up. Curl up.

Relax

Relax

Relax

Close your eyes.

Purr Purr

Purr Purr

THE END

Kitty
Tubers

Made in the USA
Coppell, TX
09 May 2023